DISNEP

HIGH SCHOOL
MUSICAL
THE MUSICAL · THE SERIES

IN THE
SPOTLIGHT

D0109070

DISNEP PRESS

Los Angeles · New York

NINI AND RICKY'S STORIES

By CARIN DAVIS

Based on the original series created
by TIM FEDERLE

Printed in the United States of America
First Paperback Edition, October 2020
10 9 8 7 6 5 4 3 2 1
FAC-025438-20255
Library of Congress Control Number: 2019957968
ISBN 978-1-368-06422-4

For more Disney Press fun, visit www.disneybooks.com
Visit DisneyChannel.com and DisneyPlus.com

SUSTAINABLE
FORESTRY
INITIATIVE

Certified Sourcing

www.sfiprogram.org
SFI-01054

The SFI label applies to the text stock

CHAPTER

01

ASHLYN'S THANKSGIVING PARTY

The last time I had thrown a party that big, half the guests were stuffed animals, which was how my favorite bunny, Fluffy, ended up with a red punch stain on her right ear. So I had been a little nervous about being able to pull it off. It wasn't exactly a rager, but, you know, I'd call Thanksgiving: the After-Party a success. It seemed like everyone had fun.

The idea for the party just kind of happened

after rehearsal on Friday. I told Carlos and Big Red that E.J.'s folks were treating my folks to some high-end spa thingy in Park City.

"Wait, do you guys want to come over after dinner tomorrow, like a late-night party?" I asked.

"I never don't want that," Carlos said.

"Should we keep it to a small group?" Big Red wondered.

"Party at Ashlyn's after dinner tomorrow," Carlos blurted out to the whole rehearsal room. "Everyone's invited!"

So, like, the whole cast and crew were suddenly coming to my house. Not that I minded. I liked the idea of hosting a big party. Isn't that a basic teenage rite of passage or something?

4

Plus, I'd already baked a bunch of pies for baking club, so I had something to serve. I mean, I didn't just serve pie. I got veggies and chips and tons of sodas and stuff. Everybody brought something, too, which was cool of them. Nini made cookies. E.J. brought lobster dip and some forty-year-old balsamic. Gina brought gluten-free cupcakes with little turkeys on them. And Seb brought fresh milk, which I guess is a thing when you live on a farm.

I also got some Thanksgiving decorations and streamers at the party store. I figured, why not lean into the whole Turkey Day theme? Hopefully everyone took the decorations in more of an ironic way, which is what I intended.

Big Red came over early to help me set

everything up. He said his folks started napping before the Macy's parade ended, so he was free. I guess because he's on crew, I figured he'd be good at carrying stuff. Also, there's something sweet and thoughtful about him, like that compliment he gave me about throwing a brighter spotlight on me because he likes the way I sing. How is that not adorkable?

"The party may begin," Carlos said as he walked into the house, carrying this crazy giant game board. "This is something I've been waiting many long years to share with the world. You guys, this is *High School Musical*: The Choosical. When I was a child, I wanted to go into the movie but the movie was on a screen, so I decided to create the next best thing: an interactive, hyperactive *HSM* experience that can be played by children and adults everywhere in the world, as long as they lived in my bedroom."

"So you've had this thing in your room for ten years?" Big Red asked.

"Yes, but I've never actually played it," Carlos said.

"We'll totally play it," I told him.

Carlos had created all these fun categories to pick from: Get'cha Head in the Frame trivia challenge, Bop to the Top dance challenge, Synch to the Status Quo lip-synching challenge, and Looking for Glee singing challenge. To move spaces, you actually had to sing and dance and stuff. Only Carlos would go to that kind of detail. It was super impressive. I joined the same team as Big Red: the South Side—I mean the West High Knights. Don't make a big deal out of it.

Usually people spend Thanksgiving saying what they're grateful for, not what they're sorry for, but somehow E.J. chose Thanksgiving to go on some kind of weird making-amends campaign. He was admitting all this messed-up stuff he had done. I guess I'm impressed with the change. My cousin is not the type to try to make things right, so this is a whole new thing. I'm not exactly sure if the world is ready for the new E.J., though.

He called Emily Pratt from theater camp and confessed that he had given her a spoiled deviled egg on opening night so that Nini could go on in her place. Then he passed his phone to Nini, which completely threw her. She was clearly not expecting to talk to the girl she had stolen the spotlight from—even if she hadn't known on opening night what was going down.

Ricky and Gina came together. He walked in wearing a hat Gina had knit for him, and the whole Ricky-and-Gina-arriving-together situation threw Nini even more. I guess it has to be kind of weird to see your first love with someone new. But hey, we're drama kids. So there's gonna be a lot of drama. I'm just glad it didn't ruin my party, because I'd call this shindig a total success.

CHAPTER 02

THE START OF SOMETHING NEW: NINI 2.0

Whoa. Emily Pratt . . . definitely didn't expect to talk to her tonight. That was weird. But nice. I mean, I didn't know if she'd ever talk to me again once E.J. told her the real story about how she got "sick" and I went on for her as Marian the librarian in the summer camp production of *The Music Man*. I wasn't sure what I was supposed to say to her.

But it turned out E.J. had done the heavy

honesty lifting. By the time he passed me the phone, he'd already confessed everything to Emily. Surprisingly, she was pretty cool about it. She seemed too focused on her new drama school to be upset about something from last summer, which was a huge relief. Theater camp was the best experience, like, ever, and I learned so much from Emily.

I've always loved singing. And acting. And show tunes. Ever since my moms took me to see a touring production of *Annie* at the Eccles Theater when I was eight, I've basically been obsessed. I pretty much know every lyric to every Broadway musical ever. Seriously, ask me to sing any show tune and I can belt it out, no problem. *Hello, Dolly!*; *Hamilton*; *Oklahoma!*;

Wicked; *The Lion King*; *Brigadoon.* Love them all. And have you heard the *Rent* soundtrack? Amazing. I know every note.

But at East High, I hadn't been cast in anything but the chorus. True, East High has a ton of super-talented students, so the leads don't usually go to freshmen and sophomores. But still, a lot of underclassmen get cast in supporting and featured roles. Or, um, you know, they at least get to say one line. I literally never got past the chorus.

My moms heard about this theater camp and showed me the website, and it looked pretty cool. And when I told Kourtney I was thinking about going, she started jumping up and down and doing that thing with her voice she does when she means business.

"You have to go, Nini," she said. "You deserve to be there with all the other talented kids."

And something inside me agreed. Four straight weeks of musical theater, doing something I love 24/7? Sign me up. Sure, of course I was hoping to land a speaking part. But I figured even if I didn't, the worst thing that could happen was I would have an epic time with new friends and end up playing the back end of a cow. Again.

Then, before I left for camp, the whole Ricky debacle went down. Writing Ricky a song to celebrate our anniversary was honestly the first idea I had for a gift for him, and it just felt right. I spent weeks composing the melody and writing, then rewriting the lyrics, getting them perfect. I knew what I wanted to say, but the tough part was figuring out how to say it. But that's part of the songwriting process, right? I eventually got it down.

Once everything clicked, I recorded it on my phone. I know, I could have sung it to him in person when we were hanging out one night, but that didn't seem special enough. I wanted it to be a big gesture for a big moment. A video seemed like the way to go. Also, I still get really nervous performing live in front of other people. So yeah, I posted it to Instagram. That's how I told him, "Ricky, I don't not love you."

I'm not exactly sure what I expected Ricky's

reaction to be. Probably like something I've seen in one of those nineties rom-coms my moms make me watch when it's their turn to pick on movie night. You know, like Ricky would sweep me up in his arms and tell me I was a crazy-talented songwriter and he didn't not love me back. But instead, he sat there and said nothing. Well, not nothing—worse than nothing.

"Oh," Ricky mumbled.

"Oh?" I managed to muster.

"It's just that's a really big thing to post online," Ricky said. "Look, I've been thinking. You're just going to be out of town for like a month, right? And you're probably going to have, like, no reception in the woods. Maybe we just chill for a minute. Like take a temporary pause."

"A pause," I said. My stomach dropped. For a second, I thought I'd misheard him. But then I looked up and saw his face and knew he'd meant it.

"Yeah, I totally get that," I said, trying to not let on how upset I was.

"I'll text you," he said. Then he hightailed it out of my room.

So, yup, I got dumped or paused or put on a break or whatever you want to call it. And instead of spending my last two days before camp chilling with my boyfriend, who didn't love me, I basically locked myself in my room and cried. I told my moms I was in there packing, but I'm pretty sure they knew the truth. Kourtney said she could hear me crying from the driveway. I was kind of devastated and suddenly really, really grateful that I was leaving town for four weeks.

Kourtney was really sweet and gave me a camp survival kit she put together herself as a going-away gift. It included a couple of peel-off face masks, because she said I had to look radiant onstage; a blue headband to keep my hair out of my face at rehearsals; neon bandages in case I got blisters from all the dance practices; and a frame with a picture of us at Spring Carnival to remind me I wasn't alone.

Kourt was going to spend the rest of her summer focusing on intersectional feminism and dismantling the patriarchy. She said I should take a cue from her and that I was better off going to camp as a single lady, not weighed down by a dude waiting for me at home, even if that dude was Ricky. I saw what she was saying, but I would have preferred it if Ricky had just said, "I love you," back. But he hadn't.

Camp sent out a whole long packing list to everyone. Jazz shoes, tap shoes, character shoes, leotards, tights, a notebook for rehearsal notes, swimsuits, flip-flops, towels, bug spray, a shower caddy, et cetera. I filled one of those giant army surplus duffel bags plus my backpack. And I brought my keyboard and my ukulele. And then my grandma gave me a totally cute monogrammed rehearsal tote filled with snacks. I tried to explain that people online said the mess hall food was pretty good, but she was having some kind of grandma moment and felt the need to send me off with rations. And it's not like I was gonna say no to red licorice, right? My moms and I, plus all the bags, crammed into the car, and we were off.

Here's the thing: I thought it was going to be hard to say goodbye to my family, but the second I set foot on camp grounds, this glittery excitement surged through me. There were people under a tree singing a *Dear Evan Hansen* medley. There were two girls debating Sondheim versus Andrew Lloyd Webber. It. Was. Ridiculous. I felt right at home.

The cabins at camp were all named after

different shows. I was assigned to the *Camelot* cabin with three other girls. Pilar and I were enrolled in the performance track, Jade was focused on choreography, and Kelsey was into set design. She showed us some of the sets she built for her school's performance of *Guys and Dolls*. She has an incredible eye. The whole cabin started talking as we unpacked. It weirdly felt like we all became instantly close, maybe because we had a shorthand. Theater people just get each other, you know?

Pilar called dibs on a lower bunk near the window, claiming something about sunlight and vitamin D, and asked if I wanted the top bunk above her. Jade and Kelsey split the other bunk. The cabins were a little rustic. There was no air-conditioning, only fans, basically zero closet space, and one bathroom for all of us to share. But it was cool and kind of drove home the whole feeling of being away at camp. Our cabin counselor, Aisha, was majoring in theater at Northwestern, which was, like, way inspiring. It got me thinking that maybe I could study theater at college, too.

Kourt was totally right—as always. That girl definitely knows me. There was no way I was going to waste this once-in-a-lifetime opportunity wallowing in self-pity because of Ricky. This was my time to chase my dreams, to be fully present and to just work on my craft. Theater camp was the start of something new.

CHAPTER

03

HOW DID I GET HERE?

If you'd asked me a couple of months ago, I never would have guessed I'd be spending Thanksgiving night at a party with a bunch of drama kids. Not that I didn't have fun. The theater kids are cool. I just mean a lot has changed since the summer. I didn't even know who Ashlyn was a few months ago, so I wouldn't have expected to be at her house. And Gina hadn't moved to town yet, so I definitely wouldn't be wearing a hat she knit me. By the way, how cool is it that she knows how to knit and can make a hat? Maybe I'm just getting to know her, but it sort of seems like something has shifted in Gina. Like she's softer somehow. I don't know, kinder. And she's making a big effort to be friends with me.

I assumed my mom would come back from Chicago for Thanksgiving, lugging a giant tin of popcorn she picked up for me from that store by her office. And then she, my dad, and I would cook a huge Thanksgiving dinner together, eat way too much, and then roll to my aunt Judy's place to eat endless amounts of dessert. I mean, sure, my folks probably would have spent most of the day arguing about how much stuffing to make and how early to start cooking the turkey, but that's normal, right? Most families get stressed out and argue on holidays. And whatever, maybe my folks got stressed out and argued on most non-holidays, too. But legally separating? It's a lot.

Corn bread is my mom's Thanksgiving specialty. When I was a little kid, we used to bake it together. She even got us matching aprons and taught me her family secret about how to make it moist. She swore me to secrecy, but I don't think it's a big deal if I tell you a little bit about why it always turns out so delicious. It's because she uses the highest-quality white cornmeal, full-fat buttermilk, and a well-seasoned cast-iron skillet. Then she serves it straight from the oven with homemade honey butter. Not to brag or anything, but it's amazing. I'm talking five-star-restaurant good.

My dad and I skipped corn bread this Thanksgiving. We ate hot wings and instant mashed potatoes. Yeah, I know, pretty lame. But I don't blame Dad; he's trying. He's just a really bad cook. And he's been on this hot wings kick since my mom left.

I called my mom earlier tonight to wish her a happy Thanksgiving. It took me most of the day to work up the courage to reach out to her. I was seriously considering sending a text, but then it felt weird, not hearing her voice on Thanksgiving for, like, the first time ever. So I called her and some dude answered the phone.

He said his name was Todd and that he'd heard so much about me. Who's Todd? And when did this Todd guy hear so much about me? How long has Mom been hanging out with him? I just want things to go back to the way they were, okay? Even if my folks were constantly fighting. It was better.

Like over the summer, a few weeks before Nini left for theater camp, my parents took us both out to Big Red's parents' pizza restaurant, Slices, to celebrate the end of the school year. It was kind of like a double-date thing. Yeah, I know, double-dating with your parents is about one of the lamest things you could do. But I didn't care. It made me happy, all of us being together. My mom and dad sat next to each other in the red booth; Nini sat next to me, holding my hand under the table. We were all laughing as Nini demonstrated how she slurps all the foam off her root beer in one big gulp. She's been drinking it like that since we were kids. I remember she did it at my birthday party when I turned eight, and then she walked around with a root beer mustache for like fifteen minutes. It made the whole class crack up.

Anyway, Slices was going pretty well until the waiter mentioned the daily special. We were all set on ordering a large thin crust with mushrooms, tomatoes, and extra cheese, so the dude didn't even have to bring up the special. But he did: it was deep-dish Chicago-style pizza. Next thing you know, my mom's telling us all about the most amazing pizza she had at this little place while she was in Chicago on her business trip. And Dad got upset and said we were going with the thin crust, like we always did. And then Mom shot him a look, and I don't think the two of them said another word the rest of the evening. It was mega awkward. But even then, even though the double date was a total disaster, at least we were all together. Isn't it better for a family to be together, even if they don't get along, than to be spread out all over the place, each doing their own thing? Me, Mom, Dad, Nini—all four of us, we're each doing our own thing now. And it sucks. I don't get it; why do things have to change?

CHAPTER

04

A HAPPY DRAMA CAMPER

I know I was pretty upset when I left for drama camp, but once I got there, camp was everything. It was like something I'd always dreamed about—but better. Every morning we had these rotating classes: scene study, vocal technique, a couple of different styles of dance, and improv. It was all really serious training that could help elevate our performances. Then, in the afternoon, we alternated between show rehearsals and typical camp stuff, like hiking, swimming, and volleyball, which, by the way, I am terrible at. Although, randomly, I'm really good at archery. Not sure why.

The camp itself was beautiful. It was set right on the lake, surrounded by trees and, like, this beautiful natural landscape. Each age group had its own cluster of cabins, and there were larger buildings for the mess hall, the theater, and rehearsal spaces. It was like its own little idyllic world, and such a nice change from Salt Lake City. It felt good to switch things up.

The best thing about camp, though, was that we lived and breathed musicals. In the morning, they woke us up by blasting show tunes over the loudspeakers. Being jolted awake at seven a.m. by "Do You Hear the People Sing?" from *Les Mis* is actually completely energizing. You're motivated all day. If those people in Paris could stage a revolution, we could definitely stage a play in under four weeks. And then, at lunch, it seemed like someone would always hum a few bars of a random ballad, and suddenly the whole table would join in, and then the whole mess hall was spontaneously belting it out. Yeah, I know, it sounds kind of cheesy, but mostly it was amazing.

But our showcase production was really the best part. The way it worked at camp was we were divided into groups and at the end of the session, each group performed a final, main-stage play. This year's plays were *Hairspray*; *Once Upon a Mattress*; *Bye Bye Birdie*; and the one I was in, *The Music Man*.

Have you ever seen it? It's so good. It's about this traveling salesman, Harold Hill, who sells expensive marching band instruments to all the kids in this small town in Iowa. And he promises he'll teach them all how to play, but he doesn't actually know a thing about music. And the town librarian, Marian, she's the only one who sees right through his act. But then she ends up falling in love with him, and he with her, and . . . well, I don't want to ruin the ending for you. You should see it for yourself. But it's basically considered a classic of American Broadway musicals.

Anyway, every camper got to be in a play, but you still had to audition for parts. And they held auditions on the second day of camp, so there wasn't a lot of time to settle in beforehand. For my tryout, I sang "Goodnight, My Someone," a power ballad Marian sings. I was totally nervous. I'd been practicing at home before I left, but so had everyone else. You should have heard some of these kids sing. They were amazing. Still, I must have made an impression on the director, because for the first time ever, I was cast in not just an actual speaking part, but a featured supporting role. They cast me to play Eulalie Mackechnie Shinn, the mayor's wife. She's in a bunch of small group numbers, has a lot of lines, and supplies some major comic relief in the show. I couldn't believe it. I messaged Kourt right when the cast list went up.

Niniukegirl: So excited! I got a great part with lines! I'm playing the mayor's wife in *The Music Man*!

Kourtneymakeuptips1: I'm not surprised. I always knew you were destined for big things!

Niniukegirl: You were right! Camp is amazing!

Kourtneymakeuptips1: You go, girl! I wish I was coming up with your moms and grandma to see the show! So proud!

Oh, I almost forgot the other part. I was also cast as the understudy for Marian the librarian. She's the lead of the entire show. That means the casting people liked me enough to consider me for the lead role but decided to go a different way, which was way flattering. The girl who got the lead, Emily Pratt, is so talented. I was hoping we could rehearse a ton together, which would have been pretty exciting.

This other pretty amazing thing happened, too. I talked to E. J. Caswell. Of course I knew who E.J. was. He's kind of a big deal at East High. He's co-captain of the water polo team and was set to be the senior class treasurer. But I mean, I mostly know him from our school plays, or more like know *of* him. He's always been the male lead since I've been going to East High. He got the second lead starting his freshman year, which is basically unprecedented. But he is the type of person you can't take your eyes off when he performs. Not just because he's gorgeous, which, obviously, he is, but because he does this thing onstage where he commands it. He draws you in with this charismatic stage presence. Like when he played Herbie in *Gypsy*. Wow. People gave him a standing ovation. So yeah, I knew who E.J. was. What I didn't know was that he went to my camp.

He caught me staring at him the first night in the mess hall. I didn't mean to; I just did a double take because I wasn't expecting to see him there.

But he smiled at me, like he recognized me, too. I thought I must be imagining it, because why would he know who I was?

But then the second day of camp, after auditions, E.J. walked up to me. I thought maybe he thought I was someone else.

"Hey, you go to East High, right?" he said.

"Yes," I said. I was so nervous I could barely talk.

"I thought so," he said, smiling that dazzling E. J. Caswell smile. "You were in *Gypsy* with me, right? You played half the horse?"

I just nodded. Good thing Kourtney wasn't there. She would not have been pleased with my total lack of girl-power presence. But I couldn't help it. I was shocked.

"You had a really strong audition today," he said. "I think you've been really undervalued at East High. I'll be surprised if you don't get a great speaking role in the production."

Then he smiled and started to walk away. "Hey, it was good talking to you," he said, turning back. "You should speak up more often. People should hear your voice."

I basically floated on air for the rest of the day. It was the best day I'd had in a long time— until the next day, when they posted the cast list.

CHAPTER

05

WHILE NINI'S AWAY . . .

Did I miss Nini while she was at theater camp? Yeah. Of course I missed her. You've seen how incredible she is. I mean, any time you hang out with Nini is a good time. It's easy with her. And she gets me.

With Nini gone and Big Red working at his parents' pizza restaurant all the time, I didn't really have anywhere to go over the summer. My folks were arguing all the time, so it seemed like

I was always leaving the house. I didn't want to have to listen to them fight. I wound up at the skate park a lot, kind of hanging out by myself.

I remember one night when my parents had been giving each other the silent treatment for two days, I couldn't deal. I really wanted to call Nini, but I figured she was busy at theater camp, so I skateboarded to Big Red's.

His basement is kind of like an escape pod. His mom is super sweet. She's always asking me if I need anything. No matter what I answer, she usually hands me a fresh-baked brownie or a warm cookie or sometimes a bowl of popcorn. And his dad isn't bad at video games, so he hangs out with us sometimes. But mostly in the basement, it's just me and Big Red goofing off. Over the summer it had also been a lot of Big Red telling me to stop moping about Nini. That she'd be back in a few weeks and then I could try to hit un-pause. That's a thing, right? Un-pause? Yeah, I'm pretty sure it's a thing. I think I've heard other people talk about it.

So this one night during what I called my parents' fortress of silence, I popped over to Big Red's, but his mom said he was running errands with his dad. I could have sat there and talked to her, but that seemed lame, so I headed to the skate park.

It was pretty crowded, since no one had to be up early for school or anything. The regulars were there. Some of them were filming their tricks, working on getting sponsors. I hung with them for a bit and worked on a couple of new things. I wasn't really dialed in, though. I took a break to just watch and checked my phone in case Nini had decided to text. She hadn't. But I did get a text from Big Red saying he'd be home around nine if I wanted to meet him at his place then.

Anyway, when I looked up, this cute girl completely wiped out right in front of me. Her girlfriend was trying to show her how to do an ollie, which is kind of the most basic skill for a beginner. She got up, so I knew she was okay. I guess I laughed a little and somehow caught her eye. She smiled. And I don't know, we just started talking. Her name was Skye—with an e. That's how she introduced herself.

She said she was new to skateboarding, which I had already figured out for myself. She had come with a bunch of her friends, who seemed to be better skaters than teachers. So I gave her a few pointers that might help her out. And yes, she was really cute, so there was that.

But honestly, it was nice to talk to someone about regular stuff: summer movies we wanted to see, who had the best burgers in town, why concert ticket service fees were a scam. We both wanted to go see this acoustic guitar thing in a few weeks. I think she was giving me an opening to ask her to it, maybe. I don't know. It was just a fun conversation.

It turned out she was a sophomore at North High. We joked about the whole East–North rivalry thing. She made a joke about it being like *West Side Story*, which is a musical, which made me think of Nini. And next thing I knew, I was telling her all about the Pause. I didn't mean for it to happen. I guess I just really needed someone to talk to. And once I started talking about Nini, I couldn't stop. It all sort of rushed out of me. I told her everything—about how Nini and I had met in kindergarten, how I had given her her nickname, and how last year I had finally gotten up the nerve to kiss her. It's possible I told Skye about the Instagram song, too.

Let's just say we went from flirting to friend zone in like two seconds. So yeah, I blew it with Skye. She mumbled something like "Well,

I hope you can win her back, and maybe I'll see you around sometime," which is basically code for "not interested." Then she went back to hanging out with her friends.

I told Big Red all about it once I got to his place. For someone who has never dated anyone, he's pretty observant.

"You know, hitting pause on a relationship is so you can date other people," he said matter-of-factly. "If all you want to do when you're around other girls is talk about Nini, then maybe you should just be with Nini."

"I guess that's kind of obvious," I told him.

"Maybe you needed to hit pause so that you could realize you don't want to be on a pause," he said.

"So you're saying that hitting pause was the best thing I could have done for our relationship?" I asked.

"I guess so," Big Red said.

Now all I had to do was let Nini know how I felt—which was great, except for one small problem: she would be gone at camp for several more weeks.

CHAPTER

06

A THANKSGIVING WITH EX-BOYFRIENDS

It's still a little weird hanging out with E.J. I mean, of course he'd be at Ashlyn's party. He *is* her cousin. And it was a theater kids' party and he's, like, king of the East High theater kids. And he loves (I mean really loves) Thanksgiving. It's his favorite holiday. So his attending the party wasn't the weird part. It's just that it wasn't that long ago that we were a thing. That's what's weird.

I didn't go to theater camp looking for a show-mance. It just happened. Like how in *The Music Man*, Marian the librarian didn't mean to fall for Harold Hill. But she did. And he fell for her—on the footbridge, of all places

How did E.J. and I start hanging out? Well, they posted the cast list on the third day of camp. I was . . . I mean, I don't even know how to describe it. There was my name, listed next to a really great role and next to the lead understudy's role. Happy doesn't start to cover it. I felt, for the first time ever, like my talent was seen.

I was waiting in line at the mess hall that night when Kourtney texted again. She wanted me to know that I was not the only one with exciting news. She, too, had a new role, as president of her new club: the Future Is Female club. One thing I know about Kourt is that when she gets an idea in her head, there's no point debating it. She said the new club, of which she was the only member, was the most important thing to happen that summer. She was making some point about how feminism started at home, and saying that clubs looked good on college applications, and that being a feminist got her out of chores and cooking around the house, which completely cracked me up. Seriously, that girl is the best. I can't believe she couldn't make it to the Thanksgiving shindig tonight. She would have loved it. And she would totally have helped things with E.J. be less awkward. But she had plans with her family, so I get it.

So E.J., right . . . our show-mance. I got Kourtney's text in the mess hall, and I was doing that thing you're not supposed to do, where you walk and text at the same time. And *bam*! I walked right into E.J.—like smack-dab into him, right in the middle of the mess hall.

In the movies, they'd call it a meet-cute. But in my life, I'd call it an embarrassing moment, except E.J. didn't make me feel embarrassed. Actually, the opposite. He acted like he was glad I had run into him. I was not expecting him to be that sweet. I was a little taken aback. I guess I assumed . . . I don't even know what I assumed. Maybe that a soon-to-be senior who always got the lead in the school play and who looked like a movie star would be on more of an ego trip? But he wasn't.

"Hey, congratulations on landing Harold Hill," I said.

"Congratulations on Mrs. Shinn and on being Marian's understudy," he said. "You know, understudies shadow the leads at every rehearsal, because it's a great way to learn and expand your craft. And with poison ivy and allergies and stuff, it's pretty common for understudies to step in. I've been coming to this camp since I was ten, and I've seen the understudy go on a bunch!"

Then we sat down and actually had dinner together. He told me he first started performing when he was like five. He came from this big music theater family, and he and Ashlyn and their other cousins were always putting on family plays growing up. Maybe that's why he's so comfortable onstage. I don't know. But then he asked me about my family, and we talked about my moms and my grandma. It was nice. It was cool that E.J. wanted to know more about me and my family. And it didn't hurt that he had a killer smile. When he smiles at you, with those eyes, it's pretty hard not to melt.

After dinner, E.J. asked if he could walk me back to my cabin. There were a bunch of kids sitting outside the *Hamilton* cabin, and they all shouted hi as we walked by. It was like E.J. was the mayor of theater camp. Everyone knew him. But he chose me to walk with after dinner. We were cracking each other up, debating the merits of "Shipoopi" versus "Seventy-Six Trombones"—which is a totally normal theater camp conversation, but I was having it with E. J. Caswell, which was a totally not normal event in my life. I kept wondering if E.J. was interested in me or just being nice to me since we went to the same high school. I could hear Kourtney's voice in my head saying, *Of course he's interested in you! Why not you?* So I went with it.

"I'm really happy that we're going to be at all the same rehearsals," he said as we reached my cabin.

"Me too," I said.

"And since you have to learn the whole Marian part, we can run lines and work on choreography and stuff together during free time," he said.

"That sounds like fun," was all I could say.

So yeah, that's how it happened. That's how our flirtship started.

CHAPTER

07

FROM SKATER
BOY TO
THEATER KID

High School Musical: The Choosical was actually a really fun game. It's pretty sweet that Carlos kept that giant board game stashed in his room for ten years. He actually found the perfect occasion to bring it out. And seriously, the guy made up his own game! Who does that? It's sort of amazing, right? He went all out with the details. And everyone was really into playing it. That's something I've noticed about theater kids that's different from skaters or the other kids I've hung around with at East High. Theater kids aren't afraid to be creative. There's no judgment. Everyone accepts you for who you are.

I'm still not exactly sure how I ended up here. I mean, dude, I'm the lead in the fall production of *High School Musical*. Troy Bolton! Me, a skater boy, full-on singing and dancing and everything. I got kicked out of *The Greatest Showman* because I kept talking in the movie theater about how musicals are not realistic. People don't randomly break into song and start dancing. I totally remember that night when Nini and I went to see the movie. We weren't dating yet or anything back then. We were just friends. We weren't driving yet, either. So Nini's moms dropped us off at the movie theater on their way downtown to meet some friends for dinner. *The Greatest Showman* was obviously Nini's choice. She'd watched the trailer a zillion times and was pretty amped to see it. I was . . . let's just say less enthusiastic. I'd never even seen *High School Musical* at that point. To be honest, the first time I watched it was in the East High computer lab the day of auditions. I knew who Zac Efron was. I knew Hugh Jackman, but from his superhero stuff. I had no clue the guy could tap-dance. It wasn't exactly a must-see movie for me. But since we were kids, Nini and I have had this thing where we alternate who gets to pick the movie. And it was her turn. So musical it was.

I couldn't resist shouting at the screen, pointing out how silly parts were. That's how we got kicked out. Nini was a little annoyed at first. But then the night turned out to be pretty fun. Nini's moms weren't picking us up for another hour, so we grabbed ice cream and walked around and talked. She's a really great listener. I told her about how my parents had been fighting a lot. I hadn't told anyone before that. Not even Big Red. I guess I thought if I kept it a secret, maybe it would go away. I think I might have been embarrassed, too. Or, like, ashamed or something. I didn't want anyone to know that things weren't ideal at home.

But that night, I blurted everything out to Nini. We were enjoying our mint chocolate chip and double chocolate brownie crunch ice cream, and the next thing I knew, I was telling her what had been going on at home. Yeah, I felt better sharing it with her. It wasn't just about getting it off my chest, but how she made me feel after I told her. She knew the right things to say and not say. And she reminded me that she had my back, no matter what else was going on. She said I could always talk to her . . . about anything. I just knew that being with Nini made me feel like everything was going to be okay.

And that's when I started realizing that I had feelings for her—that I *liked her* liked her. It took a while for me to realize she felt the same way.

Except now she doesn't feel that anymore, and it's totally my fault.

That's how I ended up spending Thanksgiving night at Ashlyn's house. I auditioned for the musical so I could be around Nini. And somehow, I actually got the lead.

Not that that's a bad thing. It's a good thing. So there I was, playing *High School Musical: The Choosical*. And me and E.J. doing the Sharpay–Ryan warm-up thing was totally awkward. But at the same time hilarious, right? And if I think about it, if I'm honest with myself, I'm into being in the play. I like being a theater kid. I'm glad Big Red and I found our way here.

You gotta admit it's a pretty great crew. Carlos, Ashlyn, Seb, and Gina, too. When Gina first arrived in Salt Lake City, she seemed pretty intense. But tonight, before the party, she told me how she has been dealing with having to move from place to place with her mom all the time. She said sometimes you have to do what makes you feel happy, for yourself. I guess I'm saying she really came through for me tonight, which I'm starting to realize is typical for theater kids. This is a loyal bunch!

CHAPTER 08

LET THE SHOW-MANCE BEGIN!

Ashlyn is seriously one of my favorite people. Her song "Wondering," the one she wrote for our production of *HSM*, is probably the best ballad in the show. She's got major talent. And she's really easy to talk to, especially about music and goals and stuff. Also, she throws a mean Thanksgiving after-party. At first we were friends just because of E.J., but now Ashlyn and I have our own thing going on.

At the party, we were in the kitchen, talking about songwriting. The thing is a lot of theater people mostly sing and dance to songs other people have written—unless you're Lin-Manuel Miranda. But that's a whole different level. In high school it's mostly about performing other people's work. But Ashlyn wants to be a professional songwriter someday, so she works at it all the time. What I love is that she has this dream and she's going for it. I told her how much I admired that, how I've never been great at going after my dreams or, you know, thinking I'm good enough to go after them. Although it has definitely gotten better since I went to camp. I came home from camp a lot more confident. Like seriously a lot more.

A big part of it, I think, is I had never studied performing the way I studied math or English, really focusing on it in a serious way as a craft, working on technique, doing characterization homework, running scene studies. At camp, they called us students of performance, which helped me a lot to reframe how I think of theater: like it's not just a hobby; it's something I'm really serious about.

Our camp acting teacher, Mrs. Darlene, spent a lot of time on what she called the actor's presence. Basically, she said, if you wrap yourself in too much of a cocoon when you're performing onstage, you might as well be singing into a hairbrush in an empty room. You have to be a butterfly and carry your performance out into the theater, flying over every audience member. That's a lot, I know. But it makes sense, at least to me. When I texted Kourtney about it, she wouldn't stop calling me a butterfly for like a week. But it's a pretty good metaphor. It's way better than imagining the audience naked, which I never really got.

Then there was the camp vocal coach, whose name was Larz. I'm pretty sure that was his theater name, but whatever. He was all about vocal projection. He'd stand way in the back of the theater and try to hear us, while insisting on no shouting. His whole thing was that improving your stage voice wasn't just about volume and breathing exercises—although we had to do a lot of those, too. We did a lot of tongue twisters and stuff to make sure we enunciated our words. In our cabin in the mornings, we used to compete in doing the Larz tongue twister exercises with a mouthful of toothpaste. Pilar was the queen at it.

"Projection comes from confidence, from believing in your own talent," Larz said. "It's almost like a reverse spotlight that starts from within you and shines out onto the audience."

I know, now I'm supposed to be a spotlight and a butterfly, but I realized these instructors were right. It all starts with you believing in your own talent. And if I was ever going to get past the chorus, I had to start believing I deserved to!

And yeah, it helped that E.J. believed in my talent, too. It gave me that extra boost of confidence. And, um, I guess it wasn't even just his believing in my talent . . . it was like he believed in me, as a person. Does that make sense? He wanted to hear what I had to say, and encouraged me to lead more when we were in a group.

Anyway, we were growing really close, me and E.J. We had classes and rehearsals together. Then we'd run our lines and staging on our own. Mrs. Darlene said that feeling comfortable onstage came from not being nervous about your lines or the choreography, that if you practiced to the point where you had no doubt about those details, you were free to just perform, let your talent take over.

So E.J. and I had this whole camp routine. We'd go to classes and then spend our free time rehearsing together. We'd eat dinner together in the mess hall, too, sometimes joined by my cabinmates. And then he'd walk me back to my cabin. One night, when he was walking me back, he grabbed my hand. We stopped by the lake. It looked so much different at night than during our daytime open swims, when it was packed with people playing Marco Polo and lifeguards whistling for buddy checks. At night, it was calm and really beautiful. So yeah, it's a little cliché, but E.J. leaned in and kissed me. As soon as he did, I got all tingly. It was like a surge of electricity through my whole body. At least, that's how I described it to Kourtney when I texted her after lights-out.

After that night, E.J. and I were a couple. There wasn't some awkward status talk or anything. It just happened. We were together. We were having a show-mance.

CHAPTER

09

RICKY
FINALLY
GETS IT!

Dude, there's no one like Big Red. He's beyond loyal and always there for me. So no, I wasn't surprised when he followed me into Ashlyn's kitchen after Gina left the party. She found out her and her mom are moving again, and she was pretty upset. I tried to get her to talk to me, but she shut me down. Big Red sensed that I was upset, too, so he came to check on me. I get it. Do I wish I could tell him everything was okay? Yes. Is everything okay? No, not really.

Big Red and I had big plans for junior year. We couldn't wait for our first day as upper-classmen. It was gonna be our year.

I remember us hanging out in his base-ment the week before school started, talking about how we were finally going to almost rule the school this year. Big Red joked that he was going to grow a mustache—which he didn't. Mostly because he can't. But his atti-tude was going to be all mustache, know what I mean?

I suppose his attitude still is. I mean, he's killing it on crew. Who knew? And no, he hasn't exactly told me he's crushing on Ashlyn, but I know he is. He did volunteer to go over there today and help her set up, and I've known Big Red for a long time: he is not the "arrive early to help" kind of guy. He's more the "stay home and play video games and then bail on the party altogether" type. So Big Red going to Ashlyn's early, that's good, right? Maybe he's about to start an epic junior-year romance. That would be cool!

But me? I thought junior year was going to be me and Nini—together. Hanging out, grabbing pizza, going to the movies, going to Homecoming, you know? Couples stuff. Because I thought we were going to be a couple. I thought we were good. We took a pause while she was at camp, and then I thought we'd pick things up where we left off once she got back.

A few days before Nini was supposed to come home, I saw that Kourtney had posted something about how proud she was of Nini for getting a great part in her camp's production of *The Music Man*.

I figured it would be the perfect time for me and Nini to hit un-pause if I went to see her perform. So I texted her to see how rehearsals were going and also to let her know I wanted to come up and see the play.

Well, actually, no, all I texted Nini was "Hi." But my plan was to tell her everything once she wrote back. I was going to admit that I'd made a big mistake, that I really missed her, and that I wanted to see her show and support her, because she's amazing.

But I never got to write all that, because she never texted me back. I told myself that she might not have gotten my text, that the cell reception up at the lake was probably really bad. And even if it wasn't bad, she was probably really busy with rehearsals and didn't have time to text back. Or maybe they weren't even allowed to have phones at rehearsals because the camp took their theater stuff so seriously. Whatever the reason, she didn't write back, so I didn't go see her show, which sucked, because I realized I really wanted to see her show. I wanted to see Nini. I wanted to give her flowers and tell her how fantastic she was up there and have her smile at me when she saw me—that smile that made me feel like we were a team.

I should have told her I loved her that night. I don't know why I didn't. I'd overheard my folks the week before when my mom was packing for some sales conference in Chicago. My dad asked her not to go. He didn't say, "Stay here and let's work on our relationship. I love you, and I know you love me." That's not something my parents ever say to each other. Maybe that's why I have such a hard time expressing my feelings. I should have told Nini why I couldn't say it and why I froze when she showed me her Instagram post.

When Nini announced she loved me for basically the whole world to see, I panicked. I freaked out. I hit pause. Okay fine, did I break her heart? Possibly. Did I do the wrong thing? Definitely.

But waiting for her to text me back that day, checking my phone every hour to see if I missed a call or something from her, I knew I had to do something to win her back. I was determined to make things right.

And then she came back from camp with a new boyfriend. Look, I know, I messed up. Big-time. And even though I thought being in the musical would help us get back together, we're still not a thing. But I know I want to be. I want our show to be a hit. I want to deliver a Troy performance that's worthy of Nini's Gabriella. And yeah, I want the show-mance.

CHAPTER 10

NINI TAKES THE LEAD

I was already having an incredible summer before our camp performance of *The Music Man.* The show was coming together in rehearsals, my cabin was on the winning team for camp-wide color wars, and the best thing was that I could feel myself becoming a better performer. It's kind of hard to explain, but I felt more confident onstage than ever before— like I had a right to be there, like I deserved to be there. I don't know if it was all the theater classes or my giddiness about being in a new relationship with a boyfriend who was always telling me I was talented and I just needed to believe in myself. Whatever it was, I felt like I was becoming better at all this. That's why I went to camp in the first place, right?

One other thing that I think made a difference was that there were all these younger kids at camp. And they looked up to the high school kids a lot. At East High, I was so used to being an underclassman and looking up to juniors and seniors. But at theater camp, the younger campers asked the older campers for help with everything—from sorting laundry to memorizing lines. One day Jade and I were in the dance studio, getting in some extra rehearsal time, and these three middle school girls came in and watched us in awe. Then they asked if we'd work with them on their numbers for their show. And then it became a regular thing: us mentoring them, helping them rehearse. And I guess at some point, I saw myself through their eyes.

Before I knew it, we were in tech week. And I know I'm biased, but our show was looking incredible. E.J. was mesmerizing as Harold Hill. Emily was nailing her role as Marian the librarian. And me, well, I couldn't wait to get onstage as the mayor's wife. Mrs. Darlene really helped me with my timing to add some comedic bits into my scenes, and they were getting bigger and bigger laughs with each rehearsal. Hearing people laugh like that, I started feeding off that energy and putting it back into my performance. One night, after our last dress rehearsal, E.J. called me a showstopper. I guess I'd found my stage presence. And me and E.J.? We couldn't have been better. He was, like, the perfect boyfriend.

Okay, so the day of the show was a blur. We were counting down until curtain, and you could feel the buzz running through camp. After breakfast, E.J. and I took a stroll down to our spot near the lake. The good thing was, while other camp couples were trying to figure out if they should keep dating long-distance once camp ended, E.J. and I didn't have to worry.

We knew we'd be together back at East High. We didn't have to think about our limited time left at camp together. We could just focus on opening night.

I admitted to E.J. that I thought I'd be more nervous, since it was my first time having a bigger role in a real production. I wasn't nervous at all. I was excited to go on. I was ready. He smiled and put his arm around me and told me I was a star. Then he grabbed my hand, and we walked to the mess hall together for lunch.

I knew something was up when I was walking back to my cabin after lunch and saw Emily sitting by the lake crying. It was a little hard to understand her through her tears, but she told me she had stomach flu something awful. I helped her up and took her to the infirmary. The camp nurse said Emily was too sick to perform. She couldn't go on that night.

That meant as her understudy, I had to go on in her place. So, uh, yeah, that happened.

Then came a flurry of "the show must go on" activity. There were last-minute adjustments to all the Marian costumes, since I was shorter than Emily. Larz reviewed all the Marian songs with me, and Mrs. Darlene took E.J. and me through a speed rehearsal of our blocking. There was hair, makeup, and mic checks. Right before the curtain went up, when places had been called and we were waiting backstage, I definitely had butterflies in my stomach.

"You got this," E.J. said, looking me in the eyes and taking my hands in his.

"I know," I said, which surprised me a little. But I did know. Something inside me knew that I could do it.

"That's my leading lady," E.J. said as he kissed my forehead. "Break a leg."

And then the orchestra played the first few notes of the overture.

There are basically no words to describe what I felt onstage that night playing Marian the librarian. It was magical and energizing, and . . . I don't know . . . it just felt right, like everything aligned. I knew right then that was where I was meant to be—up on the stage. To use

Mrs. Darlene's lame metaphor, if I was a butterfly, I flew circles around that audience. I reached people in the very last row. I felt connected to them. Does that make sense?

Oh, and it turned out E.J. and I clicked as well onstage as we did off. We'd rehearsed so much together that our scenes felt natural. And we nailed our duets. The crowd actually gave us a standing ovation during curtain call. So yes, standing up on that stage in the spotlight, I'd never felt so confident before in my life.

After the show, E.J. twirled me around in his arms, shouting, "Yes! I knew you could do it."

"That was amazing!" I said.

Then I ran to find my moms and my

grandma. I hadn't even had a chance to text them about going on as the understudy; they were so proud. Later, when I texted Kourt, she said she'd always known I was leading-lady material and was glad I finally recognized it, too.

The girl who had gone to camp that first day, who'd spent hours crying over Ricky, was a completely different Nini. The new Nini? The post-theater-camp Nini has her head in the game.

When I auditioned for East High's production of *High School Musical*, everything felt different. I was nervous. Even E.J. pointed out that I was speaking with a vague British accent, which I guess is something I do when I'm a little freaked out. But I told Miss Jenn that I was auditioning for the lead. And I wasn't thrown when I had to sing in the dark or even when Ricky showed up out of nowhere. I didn't let Gina get in my head. And I did it! I got cast as Gabriella.

And, well, here we are. We're opening the show in a few weeks. Am I nervous? A little. Excited? Definitely. Confident? You bet. Especially when I looked around the Thanksgiving party tonight. We have the best cast and crew— Ashlyn, Carlos, Seb, Ricky, Gina, E.J., Big Red. Like the song says, we're all in this together. So, um, yeah, I guess that's what I'm thankful for this Thanksgiving.

**KEEP READING FOR
A SNEAK PEEK AT**

*THE WONDERSTUDIES:
GINA AND E.J.'S
STORIES*

CHAPTER 01

PLOTTING AT HOMECOMING

I paced around my house and then I checked my phone. E.J. was late. Where was he? This was my first homecoming dance and I didn't want to miss anything.

"Gina, one more," my mom begged, taking a couple of pictures with her phone. "You look fantastic." She beamed at me. "That dress is just perfect!"

"Mom," I said, rolling my eyes. I tugged at

my new sequined dress. I had gotten new shoes and a bag, too. I flashed my mom a smile.

"And maybe one more by the fireplace?" my mom asked.

"Enough," I told her. My mom had already taken a dozen photos. "When E.J. gets here, we don't have time for more photos," I said. "We're late." I checked my phone again. "We really need to get to the dance."

I wasn't exactly sure what was going to happen once we got to homecoming. I just knew Nini would not be happy about seeing me with her ex-boyfriend E. J. Caswell. Sure, it took guts for me, a sophomore transfer student, to ask the senior water polo star and class treasurer to the homecoming dance, but it was all part of my plan. Something had to be done about E.J. and me being understudies. Sure, we could be *wonderstudies*, but we were better than that. We both wanted to be the leads in East High's *High School Musical.*

A car pulled up in front of the house and I saw E.J. He honked the horn. I grabbed my purse. "Bye, Mom!" I shouted as I headed out the door.

"Have fun!" my mom called.

I smiled. Fun wasn't at the top of my agenda for the night.

I was on a mission.

When E.J. and I walked into East High, Mr. Mazzara was sitting at the entrance to the gym, checking people in. He had a list of everyone who had bought tickets to the dance. I boldly grabbed E.J.'s hand and gave his name. Mr. Mazzara scanned the list. He looked up at me when he saw Nini's name next to E.J.'s. "Wait, when did you become Nini?" he asked.

I saw E.J. wince and then roll his eyes.

I smiled at Mr. Mazzara. "There was a last-minute cast change," I said coyly.

Want to know what happens next?
Read *The Wonderstudies:*
Gina and E.J.'s Stories,
coming soon from Disney Press.